Steve Webb

Illustrated by
Chris Mould

ANDERSEN PRESS · LONDON

First published in 2016 by
Andersen Press Limited
20 Vauxhall Bridge Road
London SW1V 2SA
www.andersenpress.co.uk

2 4 6 8 10 9 7 5 3 1

British Library Cataloguing in Publication Data available.

ISBN 978 1 78344 400 7

Printed and bound in Great Britain by
Clays Limited, Bungay, Suffolk, NR35 1ED

For all the sooopa people who live in my house.

Except the cat. The cat is an idiot.

SW

For Steve's cat.

CM

The Spangler

Spangles McNasty was nasty to everyone and everything, everywhere, all of the time.

He had a heart as cold as a box of fish fingers in a supermarket freezer, a brain brimming with badness and a head bristling with baldness.

There was only one thing Spangles liked more than being nasty, and that was collecting spangly things: shiny, sparkly, glittery, spangly things.

Of course, when he said 'collecting', he meant 'taking without asking or paying', or as everyone else calls it, stealing.

A perfect day for Spangles McNasty would start with a handful of his favourite breakfast – cold, greasy chips, scooped from a bin on the seafront so he didn't have to pay for them. He'd follow this with pulling faces at old ladies, shouting at babies and, if at all possible, farting in the local library. But, best of all, it would end with collecting something spangly on the way home.

If he could collect something spangly from an old lady with a baby in a library, whilst eating cold chips, farting, pulling a face and shouting all at the same time, it would quite possibly be the happiest day of his entire nasty life.

Sadly for Spangles, that day had so far escaped
him, but each and every morning he awoke with a
new nasty hope in his frozen-fish-finger-box heart.
'Maybe today's the day, Trevor,' he would say
hopefully.

Trevor was a goldfish. He lived with Spangles in a rusty old camper van, which had ended a long adventure-filled travelling life at a scrap yard, where it would have been recycled, had it not been for Spangles McNasty walking in one afternoon and 'collecting' it while no one was looking.

He had been doing his nasty collecting business in it ever since.

Camper vans are, of course, little completely mobile homes (like tortoises, but faster and with more seat belts). However, Spangles' camper rarely left his home town of Bitterly Bay, except when he was away on special collecting business. Nestled in a curve of coastline between the Jelly Cliffs in the north and Sandylands to the south,

10

Bitterly Bay was '**home spangly home**' to Spangles McNasty. An expression he liked so much, he'd written it with his finger in the dirt that covered his van, just above where he'd written, '**Trevor is a stinker**'.

Trevor swam in tiny contented circles round and round a small glass bowl hanging from the camper's rear-view mirror, where most people hang air fresheners shaped like Christmas trees.

Spangles kept Trevor hanging in the window of his camper van for two reasons. Firstly, so he had someone to talk to, and secondly, to watch the sunshine spangle on his shiny golden skin, which it was doing magnificently on the sunny Saturday morning our story begins.

Trevor swam on peacefully in his fish-bowl camper-van home, parked outside a newsagent's. He was as happy as a fish, as the old saying goes (well, it doesn't, but it should). Spangles, meanwhile, was inside the newsagent's,

 buying the local newspaper. He too, was as happy as a fish.

Trevor stopped swimming momentarily and watched the familiar baldy figure of Spangles approach.

Spangles strode purposefully through the newsagent's, swinging his patched-up pinstripe-suited arms and legs almost high enough to flick his threadbare baseball boots at the ceiling.

He whistled merrily at his naughty reflection in the glass door as he was leaving, wriggling his

large handlebar moustache and allowing his bushy caterpillar eyebrows a quick dance before trying to slam the shop door behind him. Rather annoyingly, it had one of those self-closing-smoothly mechanisms. Muttering something nasty under his breath, Spangles climbed back into the driver's seat of his camper and slammed that door instead. The van shook, setting off its ancient alarm, which wailed like an unhappy elephant at Weight Watchers. He then leant on the horn accidentally-on-purpose just to be sure.

The sunshine, the newsagent, the milkman,

Trevor and Spangles were all awake, but the rest of the world was still tucked up in bed, sound asleep. Well, they had been.

'**Wakey, wakey**,' Spangles said brightly, unfolding his newspaper, before turning to Trevor. 'Hello there, my spangly friend,' he beamed. 'And may I say how super-shiny you is lookin' this **beautiful sunny mornin'**!' Spangles was feeling unusually cheerful, and it wasn't just because he'd woken 146 local residents somewhat earlier than they'd like on a Saturday. He had nasty plans for the day ahead, and nothing made him happier than carefully prepared nastiness.

'Imagine when you're fully growed!' Spangles said, grinning manically at the shiny fish. He believed completely that goldfish grow to the size of

15

whales, and are, in fact, made of solid gold. 'Imagine the spangles on that, Trev!' he said, but Trevor wasn't listening, he was busy swimming in and out of his little castle, playing soldiers.

'Have you seen today's headline in the paper?' Spangles held up the front page of the **Bitterly Daily Blah Blah** for Trevor to read. Trevor said nothing. He couldn't read.

'Says here, "More goldfish thefts! Sandylands is the third seaside town to be hit by the **mysterious goldfish thief**".' Spangles chuckled to himself. 'How very strange, eh, Trev. Some people are right peculiar, ain't they? What kind of a nut box would collect shiny golden fish?'

He waited a polite second or two for Trevor's response and then shouted over his shoulder to the living area, 'All right in the back?'

There was no reply.

There was no reply because there was no one living in the living area. No one apart from 326 goldfish, and they never spoke. This was something that did not especially worry Spangles. As long as they all grew as big as whales and made him rich, he'd be happy.

As Spangles turned the key in the ignition, the engine grumbled its annoyance at being started so early in the morning. The bright sunshine streamed through the front window and shimmered on Trevor's shiny golden fins.

'Ah, Trev, me old spangler,' Spangles said, as the camper lurched down the road, coughing thick clouds of unspeakable filth from its rusty exhaust. 'This is going to be a right super spangler of a day, I can just feel it. Bitterly Bay, here we come.'

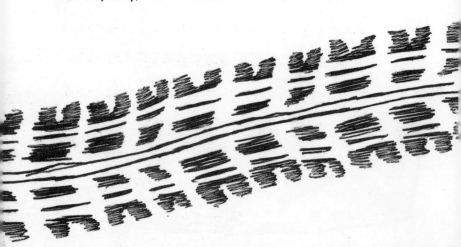

Sausage

Sausage-face Pete paced impatiently around the edges of the poop deck. (The poop deck is the actual for-real old-fashioned sailor name for the driving bit of a ship, like the flight deck on a spaceship, but not in space and less shiny.)

He was waiting for his phone to ring. He paced. He waited. He stood in some freshly squeezed bird poop.

'This ain't that sort of poop deck, you flying ratties!' he snarled, waving a fist at the seagulls circling Bitterly Harbour. Sausage-face Pete was dressed, as always, in a huge yellow fisherman's mac that covered him almost completely, with matching yellow wellies, an oversized yellow fisherman's hat and a bushy beard, which, on closer inspection, was attached to the hat by elastic.

The seagulls squawked, Sausage shouted and his phone chirped cheerily from its nesting place in the brim of his huge hat. Just why he had bird song as his phone's ringtone when he clearly hated birds, you will probably never know, unless you go to Bitterly Bay on holiday and ask him yourself.

However this is not recommended, as (a) Sausage-face Pete is as nutty as a custard sandwich, and (b) no one knows what he really looks like underneath his yellowness and fake-beard disguise. Although, with a name such as his, it is safe to assume he is not a particularly handsome man.

Sausage fished his ringing phone from his fishing hat. 'Aha! Spangles, me old glitter ball,' he answered with glee.

Have you ever heard the expression, 'There's no smoke without fire', or 'Where there's fish, there's chips', or even, 'Spangles McNasty is sure to have a nutty sidekick in a story such as this'?

Well, they're all true, especially the one about chips.

'**Good morning, Sausage**, and what a glorious day it is for collecting, eh?' Spangles shouted over the noise of the camper's groaning engine, on his hands-free mobile phone kit. (He was nasty, but he wasn't daft enough to use his mobile phone while driving). 'All set for **Operation Monkey Trousers**?'

Sausage-face Pete had been pacing and waiting for a call from his friend and accomplice in nastiness, but he was suddenly unsure it was this particular call he'd been waiting for. 'Monkey Trousers?' he replied, more than a little confused.

'Yes, yes, Monkey Trousers,' Spangles said impatiently. 'You remembers **the plan**, don't you?' he asked, emphasising the words 'the plan' as if talking to a foreigner in a foreign country where they speak foreign languages. Although Spangles had never been to any such places, he found it sometimes helped in communications with Sausage-face Pete.

'I thought we was stealing small fish made of gold that will grow as big as whales and then meltin' 'em down to make jewellery to sell to tourists from your camper van at outrageously inflated prices?' Sausage said, unrolling the contents of his confusion like a new carpet.

'Hush your **jibber jabber there**, Sausage!' Spangles snapped. 'That is exactly what we're doing, we're just calling it **Operation Monkey Trousers** for secrets, remember? In case they is listening.'

'Who? The seagulls?' Sausage stroked his fake beard, puzzling over this new information.

24

Spangles sighed, looked at Trevor, raised both of his caterpillar-sized eyebrows and shrugged his shoulders as if to say, 'What can I do, Trev? Sausage is my oldest friend and collecting accomplice, his heart is in the right place but his mind is a little muddled.'

Trevor did not shrug his shoulders nor raise his eyebrows, as he had neither.

'OK, Sausage, I'm almost there. Meet me by the Ghost Train in ten minutes, and don't forget to bring **Double Bad**,' Spangles said, and hung up.

'Right you are, me old pickpocket,' Sausage-face Pete replied, tucking his phone back into his hat and skipping down the stairs from the poop deck, the old collecting adrenaline already surging through his veins like nuclear coffee.

The Absolute Impossibility of Time Travel on a Jet Ski

The Ghost Train was at the far end of the funfair on Bitterly Pier, opposite the **Slotties Amusement Arcade**. It was one of the oldest funs in the fair, along with the goldfish and candyfloss stalls and their owner, Wendy McKenzie.

Wendy McKenzie idly twirled a finger in her curly candyfloss hair, which would have been as white as slightly sludgy snow, if she hadn't insisted on dyeing it bright pink, like actual for-real candyfloss, every weekend since she was ten years old.

She could no longer remember how old she actually was, but if you were to hazard a guess by counting the wrinkles on her face, much like the rings inside a chopped-down tree, you could quite confidently say, 'This lady is exactly six hundred and ten!'

Just don't say it where she can hear you.

Counting wrinkles on faces, although fun, is not actually a completely accurate age guide for humans, but it's pretty close and indeed proves Wendy McKenzie was the oldest lady in Bitterly Bay, and quite possibly the universe. (The next time you meet an old person – you know, older than thirteen – ask them to do their biggest smile and then count the wrinkles on their face.)

Wendy stopped twirling her flossy hair and knocked on Horatio Spectacle's door with a rolled-up newspaper.

Horatio's door flew open, revealing a small round man in a tall pointy hat, who announced rather theatrically, 'Horatio Spectacles, Fortune Teller, at your service. I can see into the past!'

'No need for the sales pitch, darling, it's only me,' Wendy said, stepping into the small wooden shack. She sat at the fortune teller's table on the customer's side. 'By the way, you really should change your catchphrase, everyone can see into the past. It's not magic.'

'Aha!' Horatio exclaimed, swooshing a dark velvet cape from a hook on the back of the door. 'But can everyone do this?' He twirled the cape around his neck, kicked the door shut behind him and leapt into the seat opposite Wendy, on the fortune teller's side.

Leaning towards the crystal ball in the middle of the table between them, he scrunched his eyes closed for six silent seconds and announced, 'Yesterday, Wendy McKenzie . . . your hair! Yesterday, your hair was pink!'

Horatio slumped onto the table, exhausted.

'Yes,' Wendy said with a sigh. 'Everyone can do that.'

'Really?' Horatio mumbled into the table, genuinely surprised.

As well as being the most senior, senior citizen in Bitterly Bay and possibly the universe, Wendy McKenzie was the funfair's oldest trader. Her candyfloss and goldfish stalls were still arranged back-to-back so she could serve both, the same as they had been the day the Mayor cut the ribbon across the now-rusty entrance gates. The only thing that had ever changed was the view. Other stalls and rides came and went on the pier, but holiday-makers never seemed to tire of candyfloss and goldfish. Not together as a snack of course.

Wendy knew everyone who worked on the

pier, and was particularly fond of her newest neighbour, young Horatio – despite his hopeless attempts at fortune telling. She tapped him lightly on the head with her newspaper.

'Have you seen this morning's paper?' she asked, slapping the **Bitterly Daily Blah Blah** down and prodding the goldfish theft headline on the front page. 'See this? Well, they don't scare me. I've never closed the goldfish stall in my life and I'm not about to start now!'

Bitterly Daily Blah Blah

PRICE 30P.

GOLDFISH STOLEN FROM SANDYLANDS' FUNFAIR

Horatio sat up. He had not known Wendy long and found each new fact about her more **alarming** than the last. 'You've never shut the goldfish stall? Not even for Christmas?' he asked.

Wendy ignored the question. 'What I came to ask you, Horatio, is this. How did they do it? How did someone steal all the goldfish from Sandylands' funfair yesterday? There's not a mention of *how*.'

Horatio grabbed his crystal ball once more, but Wendy quickly slapped his fingers with a swiftly folded paper. 'No, Horatio, you won't find the answer in there. **Think**, darling! I need to know what to be on the lookout for today.'

Horatio took a deep breath and held on to it while he thought, eyes closed again, as if searching the insides of his mind cogs.

Wendy waited. Horatio's cheeks began to turn pink. Then red. He was a dark crimson-bordering-on-purple shade when he suddenly gasped for breath and shouted, 'I have an idea! Let's ride my jet ski into the future and see what's going to happen before it happens!'

'Oh,' Wendy said quietly. 'One of *those* ideas.'

'I took her out yesterday, Wendy. We were speeding through the present, it was sooo close! If I could just get her to go a little faster . . .

. . . We'd be in the future! I just know it . . .' Horatio rambled enthusiastically.

Wendy had lost count of how many times Horatio had told her this theory. He was convinced that all jet skis could travel through time, if they reached the right speed.

'Love to, darling. If only I had the time,' Wendy said breezily, as she stood to leave.

Sausage-face Pete panted as he pedalled **Double Bad** along the promenade towards the pier. It was hard enough riding a tandem bicycle solo, but with a large tin bathtub full of water tied to the handle bars, it was nearly impossible.

He had to stand on the pedals to see over the tub and all the up-and-downy pedalling motions were sliding his hat-and-beard combination all over his head-and-face combination. Not to mention the continual sloshing he received from every bump on the pavement.

He was quite a curious sight and the early morning tea drinkers, ice-cream lickers and dog walkers began to stare. But it wasn't the bathtub-tandem oddity that grabbed their curiosity by the ears and shook it.

It was the pink beard.

Sausage had a drawer full of fake beards for special occasions. A collecting adventure such as this, he decided, needed a very particular beard. More specifically, it demanded a big, bright pink busher.

Spangles' camper van took off momentarily as he sped over the little humpback bridge on the

outskirts of Bitterly Bay. As the van clattered down
and screeched around a sharp bend in the road,
Trevor's bowl swung wildly from the mirror. The
326 goldfish sloshed around in their inflatable

paddling-pool home in the back, but no one said a word about the terrible driving. Not even Spangles himself. He was too busy counting to a 𝔪𝔦𝔩𝔩𝔦𝔬𝔫 𝔭𝔬𝔲𝔫𝔡𝔰, as that is how rich he thought he was about to become.

He slowed to a more leisurely speed on Bitterly High Street and passed babies, overflowing bins outside chip shops and even an old lady by the library, but nothing could distract him from the day's collecting plans.

Cruising past the rusty entrance gates to the funfair, Spangles' eyes swivelled to the right as he caught a glimpse of the goldfish stall halfway along the pier.

He lost count and almost crashed into a lamp post.

'**Whoopsie!** Keep your eyes on the road there, Trev,' he said to the uninterested fish. Trevor still wasn't listening, he was hiding in his castle wishing he had a telly.

On the far side of the pier, a car park stretched half the length of the beach, and was already beginning to fill with visitors. The end nearest the pier was reserved for camper vans. Spangles reversed carefully between two somewhat shinier vehicles and turned off the grumbling engine.

'**Perfect**, Trev, hidden in plain sight. Like a sausage in a pack of sausages.' He congratulated himself on his planning and hopped out of the van.

EVeryone's
a Winner

Freddie Taylor ran along Bitterly promenade as fast as his excited young legs could carry him. He **desperately** wanted a goldfish. This sudden fishy desperation had arisen from his daily dog-owning argument with his mum earlier that morning. The outcome of the argument being that if he **proved** he could look after a goldfish, she would **consider** letting him have a dog.

This was a major breakthrough in the dog-owning argument for Freddie. He had to get a goldfish immediately.

And how hard could it be to look after a fish? All he had to do was feed it and change the water now and then. 'Easy peasy,' he thought, as he ran through the funfair gates. Freddie had lived all of his young life in Bitterly Bay, and naturally had spent a lot of that young life (and a lot of pocket money) at the funfair.

'Hi, Mrs McKenzie,' he panted as he reached the goldfish stall. 'I need a fish, how much for a fish, please?'

'One pound fifty to play, Freddie,' Wendy replied, pointing to the large sign above her head which read: Everyone's a winner! £1.50

'No, I mean, to buy. I just need a fish,' Freddie tried again.

'They're not for sale, darling. You have to win one. You know the rules.' Wendy pointed in turn at Freddie, the goldfish and the sign again.

Freddie knew the rules all too well, which was what he had been hoping to avoid. He had tried Wendy's stall many times over the summers and had never won a goldfish; the sign was not entirely accurate.

He counted the two pounds and thirty pence in his hand again, as if it might have magically multiplied on the way, and gave Wendy one pound fifty. In return she handed him three small balls and pointed at the pyramids of tin cans on a shelf at the back of the stall.

It was a simple enough game. All Freddie had to do was knock down one complete pyramid with three throws. There were no tricks and no nailed-down tin cans, but no matter how hard he tried, when Freddie threw the balls, they never went quite where he wanted.

He eyed the three pyramids, chose the middle one and threw the first ball. It thudded against the wooden backboard and bounced to the floor.

He felt the eyes of 115 goldfish watching him. Hanging in individual plastic bags from the ceiling, they seemed to be saying, 'No chance, Freddie Taylor, and no dog for you.'

Wendy picked up the ball and handed it back to Freddie with a wink. 'I think you dropped one, darling,' she said kindly.

Freddie took a step to his left and threw the three balls in quick succession at a different pyramid. Two direct hits sent the top half flying, but the third missed completely.

'I think you need to change the sign,' he said, re-counting the eighty pence he now had left. 'Not everyone's a winner. How many throws for eighty pence?' he asked hopefully.

'Eighty pence, darling? You'll be asking me to give them away **free** next!'

'Well . . . if you have a spare one . . .' Freddie thought it was worth a try.

'You're as bad as the Mayor,' Wendy replied as she reassembled the pyramid of cans. 'Do you know what he suggested?'

Freddie fumbled with his eighty pence and hoped the Mayor story would have a happy ending involving a **free goldfish**.

'He asked me to go to his boat-launch ceremony thing in the harbour today, to give away free goldfish! A publicity stunt, he called it. "Good for business, darling," he said! Mad as cheese, more like!'

Freddie waited patiently. The story seemed to have ended. It didn't make a lot of sense and there was no sign of a free fish.

Wendy had put all the cans back in position now. 'Just because he's called his boat the *Fish of Gold*. I mean, what's that got to do with free goldfish? They don't grow on trees you know, honestly, some people . . .' Her voice trailed off to a whisper as something behind Freddie caught her attention.

It didn't sound to Freddie like anyone would be getting a free goldfish, in the harbour *or* the funfair, any time soon. He looked around desperately.

To get a dog he needed a fish. To get a fish he needed another seventy pence. To get seventy pence he needed . . . Aha! His eyes landed on the Slotties Amusement Arcade further up the pier, opposite the Ghost Train. 'I'll be back in a sec, Mrs McKenzie, save me a fish!' he shouted as he ran off.

But Wendy wasn't listening. She was staring, open-mouthed, at a man approaching, with a bushy, bright pink beard. 'Oh my,' she whispered dreamily. 'How wonderful.'

As he approached the Ghost Train, Freddie couldn't help thinking there was something suspicious about the strange man waiting by the exit. A bald-headed, large-moustachioed, caterpillar-eyebrow-dancing, pinstripe-suit-wearing man was sitting on a tandem bicycle with a tin bathtub tied to the handlebars. He seemed to be staring straight at Freddie, or straight through him at something further along the pier, and was muttering to himself. Freddie didn't have time to think about it though. He had a goldfish to win, so he rushed into the Amusement Arcade.

'**Spangly, spangly,** catchy monkey,' were the actual words Spangles McNasty was saying to himself, over and over again. He found this helped him stay calm when on the brink of collecting something rather special. Meanwhile his brain box raced with excitement: this haul of shiny fishes would be the last for a while. After all, when they grew as big as whales, where would he keep them? They wouldn't fit in the van for much longer, he was going to need a bigger collecting wagon.

Collecting Wagon! What a cool code name, almost as good as Operation Monkey Trousers! he thought to himself. He stopped thinking suddenly when he noticed a little girl staring at him.

'Where's the **monkey trousers**, mister?' the girl asked between licks of a dripping ice cream.

Spangles clasped a hand over his mouth.

Oops. He had a habit of doing that. Thinking he was thinking, but actually he was talking.

Was he doing it now? Hard to tell. '**Spangly, spangly**, catchy monkey,' his mind rambled, trying to calm him down.

He certainly didn't have time for a staring competition with a little girl.

'In there, shrimp,' he snapped, gesturing over his shoulder to the Ghost Train as he pushed **Double Bad**'s pedal down and rode away towards Sausage-face Pete.

Sausage was playing his part in Operation Monkey Trousers particularly well for a man with fewer brain cells than wellies. Leaning on the candyfloss counter and stroking his pink beard, he was doing his very best charming for Wendy McKenzie in his very poshest voice.

Wendy could not take her eyes off his flossy pink beard, and she twirled her own flossy pink hair with increasing speed the more the stranger talked.

Sausage-face Pete was a for-real proper sailor and had visited many foreign places where foreigners speak foreign languages, and it was with such adventurous tales he was now distracting Wendy. Distracting her so completely she didn't even notice the peculiar sight of Spangles McNasty pedalling past with a tin bathtub tied to his bicycle.

Nor did she notice when he hopped off the bicycle behind her goldfish stall and began quickly and quietly moving all 115 goldfish in their individual plastic bags into the bathtub.

Meanwhile, Wendy let slip the fact that she had **never** taken a day off work and never left Bitterly Bay, which made Sausage's job of distracting her a little easier.

'Madam,' he went on, 'you mean to say, you have never visited **Pinkland**?'

'Oh my! **Pinkland**, how exotic,' Wendy cooed.

'You poor thing! It's right next to Greenland. Of course, *everyone* in **Pinkland** has pink hair!' Sausage saw over Wendy's shoulder that all the fish were loaded into **Double Bad**'s tub. Spangles gave him the ᵗʰᵘᵐᵇˢ ᵘᵖ, hopped back on the bike and pedalled away. Sausage continued, 'And pink beards!'

'I love pink!' Wendy shrieked with delight.

'Perhaps we could go together some day, madam,' he added, tossing the end of his own long pink beard over his left shoulder. 'But for now, I must dash. Farewell, my beautiful pink lady, farewell.'

And with that he turned and ran away as fast as he could, holding onto his yellow hat and pink beard combination and leaving Wendy speechless.

'Where . . . where's all the fish?!' Freddie panted as he returned to Wendy's stall and saw the empty ceiling. He'd been lucky in the amusement arcade and had won three pounds thirty with his last ten-pence piece on a horse-racing game. This meant he had enough for two more goes on the goldfish stall, but there did not appear to be enough goldfish for even one win.

Wendy McKenzie **SHRIEKED** so loudly Horatio Spectacles came charging out of his fortune-telling shack in the middle of a reading (he was reading the paper). 'I think I just heard a pterodactyl dinosaur bird squawking from the past!' he said, scanning the sky for time-travelling birds on jet skis.

'It was Mrs McKenzie,' Freddie said.

'My goodness, Wendy,' Horatio said, seeing the empty goldfish stall. 'I think, in the recent past, you were robbed!'

'Look!' Freddie pointed at a wet bicycle tyre-trail leading away from the goldfish stall along the pier

towards

the entrance

gates.

'My goodness, I think in the recent past a bicycle has pedalled through a puddle,' Horatio stated authoritatively.

Freddie squinted at the bright blue sky. 'Except there's no rain and now there are no goldfish.'

Freddie was not a detective and had no interest in becoming one any time soon. But what he did have an interest in was getting a dog. Which meant getting a fish. Which meant he suddenly started running.

5

The Fish of Gold

Freddie followed the watery trail along the pier and out through the entrance gates, where it swerved to the right and disappeared into a wide grass verge separating the footpath from a car park. He ran across the grass and squeezed through a row of parked camper vans, only to find the car park's tarmac surface bone dry in all directions.

Meaning, Freddie reasoned quickly, the

thieves had stashed the stolen fish in a camper van and driven away . . . or, as there were no empty parking spaces, the thieves had stashed the stolen fish in a camper van and they were still in the car park. Or, the tracks were nothing to do with the goldfish theft at all and maybe he should find a goldfish elsewhere?

He examined the vans again. There were twenty or thirty of all shapes and sizes, parked side by side. Some old, restored retro-style, some painted quite weirdly, some all **shiny** brand-new, but only one, he realised, appeared to be held together by the very rust that covered it.

Freddie jogged closer and saw a ƒishbowl hanging from the rear-view mirror in the centre of the windscreen. The van suddenly started rocking as shouting erupted from within. A single goldfish swam out of a miniature castle as the glass bowl began to swing and bounce against the windscreen.

Freddie crept carefully along the driver's side of the van. There were puddles beneath his feet. He peeked through the window and listened to the rumpus inside.

Spangles was leaping up and down in the camper's cramped living area, gripping the oversized collar of Sausage-face Pete's yellow mac. Sausage quickly swapped the pink beard for the regular black busher he kept in his pocket as the two naughties faced each other from either side of the paddling pool. It now contained 441 stolen goldfish. 'We did it, Sausage! We're rich!'

'We'll be living in **golden houses** wearing **golden wellies**!' Sausage replied, ever so slightly over-excited, joining the leaping and shouting.

The thought of this particular extravagance shocked the pair into a moment's silence of wonder.

Sausage wondered if he could get a **golden hat** with a **golden beard** to match the **golden wellies**, while Spangles wondered exactly how long it would take for the fish to grow as big as whales.

'If only there were a way of speedin' up the growin' bit a bit,' he pondered aloud. 'So all these fish of gold could be fully growed right now, ready for the meltin' pot.'

A slumbering shiny fact suddenly popped to the surface of Sausage's excitement.

'**Wait, wait!** There's another! Already growed, I heard. A fish of gold as big as a boatshed!' he blurted, now grabbing Spangles' pin-striped jacket lapels.

Spangles stopped leaping and **yanked** Sausage closer, until their noses touched.

'As big as a *what* shed?' Spangles asked, his left caterpillar eyebrow trying to escape up his forehead.

'Boatshed, me old crackerjack. In the harbour. I heard that guy in the suit and hat with the giant necklace tell someone over the phone on the beach yesterday.' Sausage unrolled another carpet of facts from his brain box. 'Right **excited** he were too, about the unveiling or something.'

Spangles' right caterpillar joined the left and did a little dance.

'When you say that guy in the suit and hat with the giant necklace on the beach, you mean the Mayor, don't you, Sausage?'

Sausage nodded his head at the beachy memory.

'Tell me exactly what he said, Sausage . . . exactly,' Spangles urged more calmly, releasing his excited collar-grip and collecting his collecting thoughts as he climbed through to the driver's seat of the van.

The shouting volume dropped and Freddie could no longer hear what was being said. He slid towards the rear of the van quietly and caught sight of a familiar **bald-headed large-moustachioed** face reflected in the wing mirror.

Before the owner of the suspicious face had a chance to see him, Freddie darted behind the van, only to be engulfed in a burst of filthy smoke erupting from the exhaust as the camper's engine shuddered into life and the van drove away.

Freddie rubbed the smoke from his eyes and watched the camper lurch up the road. That was the second weird fish and gold and harbour chatter he'd heard that morning. He didn't need detective training to guess where the fishy fish **thieves** were heading next.

6

Bay Watch

Mayor Jackson adjusted his straw cowboy hat in the mirror hanging on his beach-hut office wall, finding it impossible to tell if it was the mirror that was wonky, or his hat.

He had an official office in the Town Hall, of course, with a large desk, plush carpet, two huge sofas, a giant plasma screen TV, a fridge permanently stocked with his favourite ice cream (mint choc chip) and a secretary called Marjory.

Despite these comforts, Mayor Jackson preferred his other office, the unofficial one. A small blue-and-white striped beach hut, perched in a row of other brightly painted huts at the top of Bitterly Beach. There was no fridge, no sofas or TV and usually no Marjory, but on **special** days, such as days that involved the unveiling of a brand-new tourist attraction, he liked to keep Marjory close by.

'Marjory, take a telegram,' he snapped, slapping his flip-flops on the sandy wooden floor. Mayor Jackson was a little old-fashioned and couldn't quite get to grips with the idea of email, unless he called it telegrams and thought of people on horseback galloping around the world delivering messages typed on little cards, which was pretty much how he thought the internet worked.

Marjory tried to sit up straighter in her deck-chair, not an easy task when balancing a tray of tea, extra-large chocolate muffins and a laptop on your knee. She wasn't supposed to watch online cookery shows at work, of course, but **SPOOKY COOKY** was about to start and she simply couldn't miss it.

SPOOKY COOKY was an online sensation, an almost-reality show that investigated tales of haunted food. This week's episode was called 'The Ghostly Apple Pie, the Custard and Me'.

Marjory squealed quietly with delight, 'Ooooo lawks!' before noticing the Mayor was waiting for her to do something.

'Sorry, Mayor,' she said, composing herself, fingers poised over her laptop keyboard. 'You were saying?'

'Dear Sir,' Mayor Jackson began, as he paced across the tiny room in two short strides. 'It is almost time to unveil Bitterly Bay's latest and greatest tourist attraction, the *Fish of Gold*.' He stopped, spun on a flip-flop heel and paced back again. 'The press are going to love it, and they are going to love Bitterly Bay, and they are going to **love** Mayor Jackson and Mayor Jackson **loves** Bitterly Bay and Mayor Jackson **loves** Mayor Jackson almost as much as he **loves** Bitterly Bay.'

He stopped again, facing the open doorway, staring at his beloved beach. Looking further out to sea, he noticed a gathering fog-bank, threatening to roll all the way in and ruin his day.

'Is that all part of the message?' Marjory

76

asked, clattering, *Kindest Regards, Mayor Jackson* into the keyboard. 'Who are we sending it to?'

'What?' The Mayor seemed to snap out of a daydream. 'Oh, er . . . send it to me, it's my speech for the boat launch at the boatshed later this morning.'

'Needs a little work . . . **EEEEEEEEK!'** Marjory shrieked suddenly as a photo of a rather sloppy-looking haunted apple pie filled half of her laptop screen. She clicked send.

'Speaking of which,' the Mayor said, distractedly stuffing papers from his small desk into a huge plastic beach bag, 'we should be getting over there now, final preparations, quick rehearsal and all that. It's almost time!'

Marjory couldn't take her eyes off the screen. The presenter of **SPOOKY COOKY** was taunting the haunting. 'Who's a naughty ghostie?' he said, poking the apple pie with a long stick from a safe distance.

'Maybe I should look after things here,' she offered, closing one and a half eyes as the lady who had discovered the haunted pie fainted and fell **face-first** straight into it.

'Good idea. See if there's anything you can do about the fog, will you, and just work up that speech a little and telegram it over. With an ice cream.'

'Mayor, you can't really *do* anything with fog, and you certainly can't telegram . . . I mean, email, you can't email ice cream. It doesn't work like that,' Marjory replied.

'Really?' Mayor Jackson's thoughts puzzled at the wonders of the modern world. 'Put that in the speech, Marjory: *You can't email ice cream, but you can buy one on the* Fish of Gold *as you sail around the bay!*' He carefully placed the heavy official Mayoral Chain over his head and checked it in the mirror. 'How do I look?'

Marjory glanced up from **SPOOKY COOKY** at the Mayor standing in the doorway in his flip-flops, straw hat and sandy suit with matching bling accessories, clutching his overflowing beach bag. 'Refreshingly un-dead,' she said. 'I mean, alive. That is to say, you're not dead and nor are you a ghost. Or a pie.'

'OK. Erm, thank you, Marjory,' the Mayor said cautiously, noticing there was definitely something odd about Marjory's behaviour lately, something quite creepy and he didn't like it one bit and it was beginning to give him the hooba-jarbars, or was it the heebie-jeebies? Whatever it was called, it felt like a feeling of irrational nervousness for reasons he couldn't quite put his finger on.

He decided to do what he did best in such situations: run away.

Mayor Jackson turned and leapt out of his office and collided with a young boy running towards him. They both went flying. Freddie flew further from the impact, but was back on his feet much quicker than the Mayor.

'Mayor Jackson,' Freddie panted, picking up the Mayor's hat, 'I need to speak to you, it's urgent.'

'You're supposed to make an appointment, young man.' The Mayor collected his scattered papers and stuffed them back in the beach bag. 'With Marjory.'

He gestured towards his secretary, who was now hiding behind her muffins.

'It's about the fish thefts . . .' Freddie tried to explain.

Mayor Jackson snatched back his hat and began marching towards the promenade and a waiting limousine. 'I haven't time for that nonsense now, I have a boat to launch.'

'That's what I need to talk to you about,

Mayor, they think it's a fish!' Freddie shouted after him, realising how odd the sentence sounded only after he'd said it.

The Mayor gave Freddie a quizzical look, shook his head and said, 'You young people get some funny ideas off the inter-nets, don't you?'

Before Freddie could reply, the Mayor was safely beyond reach, behind the tinted windows of his limousine, slamming the door and frowning at the approaching fog as he was driven away.

Freddie ran quickly back to the Mayor's beach hut to tell the whole story to Marjory, but found a locked door, a sign reading, 'Closed' and a lot of screaming and nervous giggling coming from inside.

Look at the Spangles on That

By the time Spangles McNasty and Sausage-face Pete arrived at the small side door to the boatshed, Sausage had revealed several more facts to Spangles.

Amongst these were: Sausage-face Pete, along with the rest of Bitterly Bay's harbour dwellers, had access to the boatshed for repairs, and the boatshed was a large wooden building with water inside instead of carpets. This bit baffled Spangles, but he went along with the idea as it meant the third and most important Sausage-fact could also be true, and that was this: the Mayor was secretly keeping a fully grown, whale-sized goldfish in the boatshed.

Sausage turned his key in the lock and pushed the creaking door open. 'Hush your **jibber jabber** there, Sausage!' Spangles urged, as they tiptoed inside. 'We don't want any of that lot knowing we're here.' Spangles nodded towards the journalists and photographers who were gathering in the harbour.

The bright sunny morning had given way to fog, which meant it was pretty gloomy outside and almost dark inside the boatshed.

'Why have they come to take photos of the fog anyway?' Sausage whispered.

'Beats me, Sausage. Weirdie beardies the lot of 'em. No offence.'

'None taken, me old fruit pie. This beard's not real anyway, look.' Sausage pulled his fake beard away from his face, stretching the elastic attachments and pulling his hat down even further over his eyes. Spangles had known Sausage since he was eleven years old and had never once seen him without a full, **bushy beard**.

The sight of his baldy

chin came as

quite a shock.

Spangles couldn't take his eyes off it and accidentally walked straight into a low wooden beam, banging his baldy head. 'Ow,' he growled through gritted teeth. 'If only we had a torch app on a mobile phone.'

Which reminded Sausage, he had a torch app on his mobile phone. One quick fumble and click later, the torchlight illuminated the dark inside of the watery shed and Spangles' angry face. 'Are you sure about this, Sausage?' he **growled**. 'I don't hear any golden whales splashin' about.'

Sausage shone the light along the walls and the boatshed's huge sliding front doors, which were closed. There was a wooden walkway leading around the edges of the shed and another dividing it into two large bays. The bay nearest Spangles and Sausage was empty. The other was hidden behind makeshift wooden panels.

Spangles was about to leave. He didn't like un-spangly things, people or places and he didn't like banging his head on things he couldn't see, and worst of all he got **bored, bored, bored** very quickly in the dark. 'As bored as a ladder,' he would have said if he'd been in the mood, but he wasn't so he didn't. Spangles felt sorry for ladders, they never got to climb on anything.

Instead he said, 'I think, what we 'ave 'ere, Sausage, is what we in the spangly trade call "a dark room full of water".'

But Sausage wasn't listening, he was walking quickly over to the fenced-off bay. 'Those big slidey doors over there, me old light bulb,' he said, flicking the torchlight across the water to the boatshed's main entrance. 'They don't go under the water, they don't need to, see. They stops at the surface.'

Spangles merely stared at his friend, wondering whether to leave immediately or throw Sausage into the harbour first and then leave.

Before he could make up his mind, Sausage continued, 'It could just swim out, see. Under those doors, into the harbour and escape. Unless you made a new fence that went right down to the bottom.' Sausage shone his torchlight along the new fencing, the bottom of which did indeed disappear under the water's surface.

A light bulb popped on in Spangles' darkened thoughts. 'Oh!' he said, eyes wide and eyebrows dancing. 'So the Mayor built this fence –' he was running now – 'to keep his fully growed Fish of Gold inside!'

Mayor Jackson cursed the fog and ushered the journalists closer to the boatshed. They could still get some decent photos from the floating jetty when he opened the doors, but there was no point taking them out on the *Fish of Gold* around the bay today, that would have to wait. He tried phoning Marjory again to make the necessary rearrangements but there was still no answer, and no sign of his speech telegram or ice cream. And **the fog**! Why hadn't she cancelled the fog? He almost threw his phone into the sea in frustration, but thought better of it.

To the Mayor, this was still going to be a great day for Bitterly Bay. The *Fish of Gold* was Bitterly's best-kept secret — hidden behind his fence in the boatshed — the biggest and best passenger speedboat in the country, not to mention the goldenest. He made a mental note to ask Marjory to thank her brother again for the paint; it really did look like gold.

Freddie ran all the way back to the funfair only to find Wendy and Horatio exactly where he'd left them, still puzzling over how the thief had done it without them even noticing. Horatio was trying to explain that his vision of the past was being blocked by the trauma of the theft itself.

'Your **goldfish**, Mrs McKenzie, I know where they are,' Freddie interrupted. 'Almost.'

'Almost?' Wendy squinted at Freddie as she twirled her pink hair around her finger.

'There was a bald-headed, large-moustachioed guy on a tandem bike with a bathtub tied to the handlebars by the Ghost Train earlier, and I'm pretty sure he has the fish in his camper van. Which is probably near the harbour by now because I'm also pretty sure that's where they've gone, to steal the Mayor's *Fish of Gold*,' Freddie explained as quickly as he could.

Wendy glared at Horatio, pointed at him and then the sign above the door to his fortune-

teller's shack, which boasted *I can see into the past.*
'Really?' she scowled, folding her arms.

'I've had an idea!' Horatio exclaimed, in a sudden attempt to redeem himself. 'We could sail into the past on my jet ski and catch the thieves red-handed!'

'Hmmm, one of *those* ideas,' Wendy replied thoughtfully. 'A slightly better idea would be to sail to the *harbour* on your jet ski and catch the thieves red-handed.'

'OK,' Horatio agreed, relieved that the scowling and pointing had stopped. 'Follow me.'

Moments later, Wendy had closed her funfair stalls for the first time ever, and was squished between Horatio and Freddie as they sped across the bay on his jet ski.

96

Spangles and Sausage quickly found a door in one of the fence panels, but it was **locked**.

Spangles turned his attention to the nearest workbench, grabbed two screwdrivers and handed one to Sausage. 'I really don't think this is the key to that lock,' Sausage said, pointing one at the other.

'It ain't. It's a screwdriver for removing those hinges,' Spangles replied, pointing his own screwdriver at the large hinges holding the door in place. One twisty, grunting minute later, the hinges were on the workbench and the door was on the floor. Spangles and Sausage popped their naughty heads through the door-less doorway.

'That's the strangest fish I ever saw,' Sausage observed after a moment's stunned, torch-waving silence. The *Fish of Gold* was a large metallic creature, floating on top of the water. It had smooth golden sides and on closer inspection, Spangles counted four circular windows.

'What kind of a Mayor puts windows in a fish?!' he muttered, horrified.

'And railings . . . and he's painted *Fish of Gold* in fancy swirly letters along the side . . . and a wooden boarding ramp.' Spangles walked along the side of the *Fish of Gold* and across the ramp. 'Oh,' he said at last. 'It's not a fish.'

'That's because it's a boat, me old anchor man,' Sausage observed.

'But look at the spangles on it! It's solid gold! Think you could **drive** it?' Spangles asked.

Sausage tried the door to the poop deck. It wasn't locked. He stepped inside and examined the controls. 'Like riding a golden bike,' he said, reaching for the ignition switch.

'Hold that **jibber jabber** a sec, Sausage.' Spangles collected his collecting thoughts once more. 'I'm having a **new idea**! Follow me.'

8

All Aboard

Spangles and Sausage wrestled the paddling pool out through the side door of the camper van, being careful not to spill any goldfish, and poured the whole lot into the bathtub, still tied to **Double Bad**.

'What's an unveiling, then?' Sausage suddenly asked, this last fact crossing the finishing line of his mind box long after the others had completed the race and gone home for a shower and a lemonade. 'That Mayor guy was proper excited about his "unveiling ceremony" on the phone.'

Spangles closed the camper door carefully, not wanting to set the alarm off this time, and swung a pin-striped leg over the front seat of **Double Bad**. 'Well, it's an erm . . . lady at a wedding,' he explained, slightly embarrassed to be talking about such private matters. 'When you marry one, they wears a veiling, and then they does the unveiling in the church. Like a sudden, ta-dahh, look at the **spangles** on this!'

Sausage joined Spangles on the tandem, scratching his confused head. 'So, the Mayor is marrying his boat?' he asked.

They heaved the bicycle into action and

pedalled back towards the harbour. The true meaning of the Mayor's unveiling suddenly hit Spangles like a fish in the face. 'The Mayor's going to unveil the *Fish of Gold* to all those photographers!' He shrieked at the realisation that the unveiling was nothing to do with weddings and more about showing off golden boats. 'Probably take 'em for a spin around the bay in it! In *my* boat! Faster, Sausage, faster, we've got to get back before they does the **unveiling**.'

Luckily it wasn't far, as they'd parked the camper only a few streets away, between two skips overflowing with rubbish — another perfect disguise. Spangles was certain it wouldn't be discovered for days, while they made their escape in his new collecting wagon: the *Fish of Gold*.

They pedalled as hard as their naughty legs could go, splashing away along the foggy promenade. Away from the rusty camper van and away from Trevor, still swimming in contented tiny circles, oblivious to the extraordinary stroke of luck that had just befallen him. He was no longer headed for the melting pot with the other 441 stolen goldfish. He was free to live the rest of his life trapped in a little bowl hanging from the rear-view mirror of a rusty old camper van.

Precisely two minutes and fourteen seconds later, **Double Bad** flew through the boatshed doorway with barely an inch to spare either side of its sloshing bathtub cargo, and rattled along the wooden walkway, skidding to a halt by the now door-less fence.

Together, Spangles and Sausage squeezed **Double Bad** through the gap where the door used to be and pushed her over the boarding ramp onto the *Fish of Gold*.

They untied the tub and quickly carried their treasure to the safety of the poop deck. 'Start 'er up, Sausage, before they sees us!'

'Who? The seagulls?' Sausage replied, already at the controls, jabbing the ignition switch with an impatient stealing finger.

A flash of light illuminated the gloom as a row of computer screens awoke, demanding a password was entered before the engine could start.

'Any ideas?' Sausage shouted to Spangles, who was busy on deck, untying the boat from its moorings.

'What?' Spangles replied, struggling to hear over a loud whirring and clanking noise that had begun whirring and clanking nearby.

With the last rope uncoiled, he ran to the boarding ramp and dragged it on.

'The password?' Sausage shouted again, watching the cursor on the computer screen blink expectantly.

'Flippin' thing, heavy as a hippo in a hairnet!' Spangles grunted.

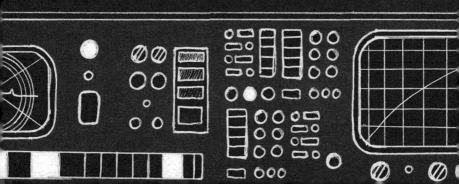

Sausage quickly typed FLIPPIN' THING, HEAVY AS A HIPPO IN A HAIRNET on the keyboard, and hit *Enter*.

The computer responded with a new message: PASSWORD INCORRECT. TWO MORE ATTEMPTS PERMITTED.

'Nope. Two more goes,' Sausage warned as Spangles joined him at the controls.

A stronger flash of light lit the room, and then another. And another. This time they were coming from outside. Spangles looked up and saw, to his **HORROR**, the boatshed's huge sliding doors were being slowly dragged open by a rather noisy whirring and clanking electric pulley system.

Above the drone and beyond the doors they heard the Mayor shouting in the fog- and photographer-filled harbour, 'Ladies and gentlemen, I present to you, Bitterly Bay's finest attraction, the *Fish of Gold*!'

'Try, "Fish of Gold"!' Spangles grinned, his nasty caterpillar eyebrows doing a quick celebratory jig across his naughty forehead.

The computer responded with a second, similar message: Password incorrect. One more attempt permitted.

'Hey! You there. What do you think you're doing?' the Mayor shrieked as the opening doors revealed a rather nasty surprise. A nasty surprise, he quickly concluded, that could only mean one thing: 'They're stealing my boat!'

The photographers' snapping and flashing suddenly intensified at the unveiling of a completely different and far more exciting story.

The Mayor **ran** up the steps from the floating jetty and along the harbour towards the boatshed's side door, closely followed by a pack of eager photographers and reporters.

Although Spangles had moved the boarding ramp, the gap between the *Fish of Gold* and the wooden walkway was easily jumpable, especially by an angry Mayor. The Mayor led the charge into the boatshed, yelling, '**STOP! THIEVES!** That boat is the property of **Bitterly Bay**!'

With only seconds to spare, Spangles rattled the words *Bitterly Bay* into the keyboard and hit *Enter*.

The engine roared its acceptance of the correct password, Sausage thrust the throttle lever forward as far as it would go. The *Fish of Gold* shot out of the boatshed, through the harbour and into the foggy bay, where it almost capsized an approaching jet ski.

The jet ski hit the boat's wake and flew skywards, with its three intrepid passengers, Horatio, Wendy and Freddie, clinging on. Two of them hoping they didn't get too wet, and one shouting, 'This is it. The future, here we come!'

As they splashed back down, miraculously not too wet, and predictably still in the present, Freddie caught a glimpse of the offending boat's name, through a wispy gap in the fog.

'Follow that boat!' he yelled from the back of the jet ski. 'It's the *Fish of Gold*, and I bet your fish are on board.'

This did not seem a particularly nutty notion to Horatio, so he spun the jet ski in a tight circle, followed in the boat's wake, and accelerated, hoping if he wasn't already in the future, he could leap there any second and see how things turned out.

Fog

Fog is a curious business. Some people say it's thick clouds that don't know where the sky is. Other people say it's just clouds that are scared of heights.

Either way, it's not the most popular flavour of weather. It doesn't make most people run up a long spiral staircase waving their arms about with excitement.

But Philip Go-Lightly wasn't most people, and that is exactly the effect foggy weather had on him. Luckily for him, he owned a lighthouse with a long spiral staircase. (A lighthouse being a tower-like building designed to shine a bright light to guide ships in danger. Not a house that isn't very heavy.)

As a lighthouse keeper, Philip Go-Lightly knew plenty about the fog business, and for Phil, fog was fun.

Which would have been a fun thing to say if only Philip Go-Lightly would speak, but he wouldn't so he didn't. Philip was a recluse and hadn't spoken a single word to anyone for fifty years.

He had lived by himself, manning the lighthouse on the tiny island of **Rock Bank**, north-west of Bitterly Bay, for all of those fifty years. He liked living alone because he liked the peace and the quiet and the view and the little private beach he had all to himself all of the time.

But mostly he liked it because of the not saying a single word to anyone, and if he continued not saying a single word to anyone for just one more year, he would break the 'Not talking for yonkers record' set by Old Man Humphrey of Humphrey's Lighthouse. Then he would get to have his lighthouse named after himself too. Philip's Lighthouse. He liked the sound of that. Not that he would ever say it, of course.

Philip's favourite part of the job was checking the light when the fog was particularly foggy. He didn't really need to climb all 350 steps up to the lighting platform to do so, but he always did. The light was indeed switched on and rotating as it should. Philip glanced through the window to see if he could see the sea from the top of his lighthouse. He could not.

He hopped up onto the handrail of the 350-step spiral staircase and slid all the way down, waving his arms above his head and miming a

silent scream as he whooshed to the ground floor.

When he got to the **bottom**, he immediately started

running back up. There wasn't a lot else to do.

Being an old **sea dog** (or an experienced sailor as some people prefer to pronounce it) Sausage-face Pete had sailed through plenty of foggy weather in his time, so he was not especially worried that he couldn't see the sea, in fact he was in such a good mood, because he'd just stolen a boat made **entirely of gold**, he began to sing one of his old sea shanties. (A sea shanty being a song sung *only* at sea by humans. There are, for instance, no desert shanties sung in deserts by camels.)

Ohhhhh . . . Hats and beards and wellies and fish!
Hurrah! Hurrah!
Cats with beers watch tellies and wish!
Hurrah! Hurrah!
They wish they had fishies on dishes like Chris's,
Chris is a cat from the circus you see.
Actually he's a lion and they don't eat fishies,
They prefer burgers in trees with peas.
So they allllllllll ran off to the pub,
Never to be seen againnnnnnn!

Spangles McNasty, on the other hand, found

his mood a rare combination of delight and fury.

Delighted at the day's collecting, even if the *Fish of Gold* had turned out not to be a fish at all, but a large golden boat, and furious at the weather for being so dull and gloomy. There wasn't a single beam of light to spangle on any of his collected treasures.

He growled at the gloom through the poop deck window, his spirits refusing to be lifted even by Sausage's beautiful song.

Suddenly, he saw a ray of hope in the fog. On the horizon, the sun winked at him cheekily and was gone. After a moment's pause, it winked again.

'**Sausage!** There's a new sun an' it's winkin' at me,' he said, pointing ahead at the light. 'It's a sign. Let's get over there quick sharp and let her shine on our spangly new Collecting Wagon.'

Sausage kept singing. He knew plenty about sailing and boats and fog and he knew a lighthouse when he saw one. But he was in such a good mood, he didn't want to spoil Spangles' fun. If Spangles McNasty thought he'd found a new sun and it was winking at him, then that was fine by Sausage. He gave Spangles a quick double thumbs up, adjusted their course slightly, pointing the *Fish of Gold* directly at the new sunshine, and added a new verse to his song:

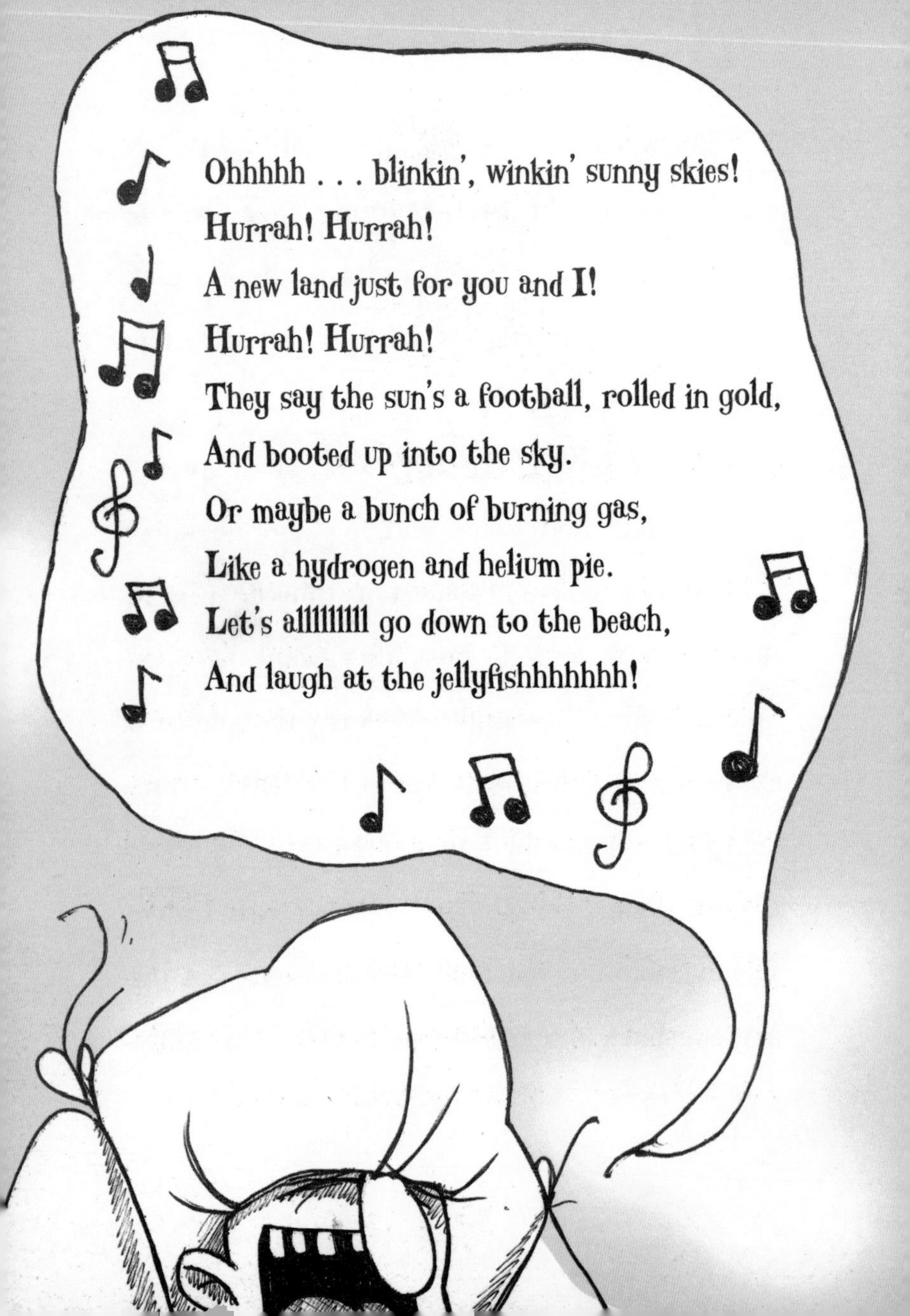

Meltdown

Philip Go-Lightly was on the beach, taking a break from sliding, when he heard the boat approach. This was unusual as it wasn't delivery day and he wasn't expecting visitors as he never, ever had any. A quick deduction meant it could only mean **one thing**. There was a boat in **PERIL**, lost in the fog on the high seas, seeking refuge on his island. In his lighthouse. *Oh dear*, he thought, *I don't like people*. And he hid behind a rock.

Sausage-face Pete expertly moored the *Fish of Gold* at the small jetty on Rock Bank. He was about to hop ashore when Spangles grabbed his oversized yellow collar and cautioned, 'Careful there, Sausage, this is a foreign land filled with foreigners who speak foreign languages. They could be pirates, or cannibals, or **stamp collectors** or anything!'

When Spangles talked like this it always gave Sausage the fear. Up until that moment, he had been pretty certain they had landed at Rock Bank Lighthouse.

'What sort of country has its own sun?!' Spangles jabbed an accusing finger at the light blinking above them.

Sausage recoiled as the light **swooped** round

again. He **grabbed** Spangles' jacket lapels, the fear already filling his wellies and rising upwards, like a Sausage-face-Pete-shaped jelly mould filling with **wibbly wobbly** fear-flavour jelly.

They were nose-touchingly close. 'What are we **to do**, Spangles? We mean no harm, we're just a couple of friendly collectors from across the sea,' Sausage stammered.

Spangles glanced back to the poop deck on the *Fish of Gold* and pulled Sausage closer still, squishing their noses together as he whispered, 'We're not welcome here, Sausage, and we're not welcome back there either. We're on the run!'

'On the run with a bathtub full of sloshing precious treasure,' Sausage worried aloud, peering along the fog-and-sand-covered beach.

'We won't get far on the sand on **Double Bad**.' Spangles' mind cogs whirred and jammed in panic, and he thought his brain might melt. '**Meltdown**!' he suddenly barked, releasing Sausage's mac.

'If we melt down the fish now, we can carry the gold in our pockets and mingle with the foreigners of this foreign land like ordinary **not-on-the-run** folk. We'll blend in, like sausages in a pack of sausages, Sausage.'

'But the goldfish will grow as big as whales if we wait!' Sausage put forward a surprisingly good counter-argument, although, like Spangles, he hadn't really considered how they would transport 441 solid-gold whales.

Philip Go-Lightly listened to this strange chatter from behind his rock and wondered if the fifty years alone had sent him mad, or if he was being invaded by dangerous weirdies. He quickly decided on the latter, and even more quickly concluded the best thing to do was to continue hiding.

Spangles had made up his troubled nasty mind and was already striding up the beach in search of firewood. He found plenty of fog, but nothing else.

'Bring that torchlight, Sausage, I can't see a **thing**.'

From behind his rock, Philip nodded his agreement. *At least the weirdie invaders understand the fog,* he thought. *Perhaps I could negotiate with them, although, I'd have to talk to do*—

'OWWWW!' Philip suddenly screamed as Spangles stood on his foot.

'AGHHH!' Spangles suddenly screamed as Philip jumped up from behind a rock, hopping on his left foot and clutching his right.

'OWW! OWW! OWWWW!' Philip repeated, listening intently to the sound of his own voice for the first time in fifty years.

'All right, all right, Mr Foreigner. It didn't hurt that much,' Spangles said, not exactly apologetically.

'FIFTY YEARS! NOT A WORD! NOT A SINGLE ******** WORD!' (Luckily for us, dear reader, the foghorn of a passing ship blasted at just that precise moment, so we shall never know what Philip's first swear in fifty years was.)

Sausage ran up the beach to join them, waving his torchlight as he stumbled over the soft sand. 'Hush your **jibber jabber**, Mr Foreigner!' Spangles tried again. 'We can make it worth your while,' he offered to no avail. Philip was enjoying himself, and he wasn't about to stop for these two **weirdies**. 'Fifty years! One more year and I'd have had the record!'

'This is a strange land and no mistake, me old deckchair,' Sausage said, pulling Spangles away from the strange stranger. 'Get the fire started with these.' Sausage fished matches and firelighters from deep inside his mac's pockets. 'A sailor is always prepared,' he added, pulling a self-inflating sofa from the other pocket and plonking it in the sand. 'Might as well be comfy. I'll get the firewood.'

It's About Time

'I think the fog slowed us down, or we'd definitely have reached **time-jump speed**,' Horatio shouted into the spray, as the jet ski sped on. 'Unless it's foggy in the future too?'

'We've lost them,' Freddie replied, dejectedly. 'The sea's too calm, we're not in their wake any more. Where are we?'

'Out by Rock Bank.' Horatio recognised the lighthouse flashing nearby. 'Philip Go-Lightly's place. I see from the past, he hasn't spoken a word for **fifty years**.'

The jet ski slowed as Horatio began turning a wide arc to head back towards Bitterly Bay.

'Horatio, darling, will you please stop that nonsense. Everyone knows Philip Go-Lightly, the lighthouse recluse, hasn't spoken a word for fifty years,' Wendy said wearily.

Before Horatio had a chance to reply, an unseen voice drifted through the fog. 'You can put that out for a start! Invading my beach, stamping on my feet, lighting fires with my wood! It's all mine, and it would've had my name on it, if it hadn't been for you two idiots! Philip's Lighthouse! Philip Go-Lightly's lighthouse!'

The owner of the voice sounded pretty angry.

'We must be in the future!' Horatio almost burst with excitement as he turned the jet ski towards the lighthouse and accelerated again. 'If he's started talking, we could be fifty years in the future!'

'Or, we could be in the present,' Wendy added flatly.

'Nope. We did it, we're definitely in the **future**, didn't you feel it? Must have been when we jumped, way back there, and then we lost the boat's wake because we're in the **future** and the boat isn't.'

This confusing explanation was confounded further as the jet ski pulled up alongside the *Fish of Gold* at the little jetty on Rock Bank.

'Care to explain that?' Wendy teased.

'They're here.' Freddie hushed for quiet. 'And if they're here, so are your ᶠⁱˢʰ.'

The boarding ramp from the *Fish of Gold* suddenly bounced and groaned under the weight of the bathtub as Spangles and Sausage carried it onto the beach.

Freddie, Wendy and Horatio ducked against the side of the golden boat in the fog, watching the silhouetted figures in silence.

'We should melt the boat too,' Spangles said.

'Don't be daft, me old hot pot,' Sausage replied. 'How would we **escape** without the boat?'

'We can walk, with our pockets full! Just look at the size of it, Sausage, all that gold!'

'My pockets are pretty big, me old treasure chest, but I doubt I could squeeze a **boat-sized** gold brick in there. Besides, the fire's nowhere near big enough. Let's just do the fishies first eh? And then see.'

Unusually for Sausage-face Pete, he was talking a lot more sense than Spangles. Although, to the six ear-wigging ears hidden in the fog by the boat, he made no sense at all.

'What on Earth are they talking about?' Wendy wondered aloud. 'Do what to the fishies?'

Freddie and Horatio were a step ahead of Wendy and shared an eyebrow-raising look of alarm.

'Wendy, please don't panic when I tell you this,' Horatio began calmly. 'Sometime in the near future, those two gentlemen are going to melt your fish on that fire,' he explained, pointing at the distant orange glow.

'But you can't melt fish,' Wendy said uncertainly.

'No. But you could try.' Freddie completed the jigsaw in Wendy's imagination for her.

'The little ***** *******!' Wendy whispered

in horror as another perfectly timed fog horn blasted somewhere out to sea. 'Leave this to me, darlings, I have just the thing,' she said, opening the rucksack she'd brought with her.

'What do you think you're doing with that then?' Philip Go-Lightly sang at the top of his voice, as Spangles and Sausage staggered and sloshed up the beach with their treasure.

'OK, we'll just do the fishies,' Spangles agreed with Sausage. 'The sooner we get it done, the sooner we can get away from this nutter.'

They flumped the heavy tub down in the sand by the side of the fire. 'If we drain all the

water out we'll have the perfect meltin' pot!'
Spangles said and started scooping handfuls of
water from the tub onto the beach. Sausage knelt
at the opposite side, pulled a large measuring
jug from inside his mac, and began sloshing
water and goldfish into both of his huge pockets
with alternate scoops.

'Where did you get that
from?' Spangles asked,
surprised at his friend's
uncharacteristic
helpfulness and
good sense.

'A fisherman is always prepared, me old lobster pot, now help me get these fishies into my mac, then we can get the tub good an' hot on the fire before we throw 'em in!'

'I hope there's chips, there's chips!' Philip sang. 'Wherever there's fish, there's chips!'

'Look, Mr Foreigner.' Spangles stood up, and spoke almost politely to Philip Go-Lightly. 'Could you please just leave us alone for a **few minutes**. We have some important business to attend to here. We appreciate your patience and apologise for any inconvenience caused. Normal service will be resumed as soon as possible.' Some of this speech, he remembered from roadworks signs he'd driven over recently.

Philip was enjoying his new-found talking so much he'd forgotten all about listening, and said, 'Ooh! I've got chips in the **freezer**! Tell you what, you do the fish, I'll bring the chips. We can have a picnic!' And with that, he disappeared into the fog towards his lighthouse.

Wendy had practised assembling her portable candyfloss kit with her eyes shut so many times, a little gloomy fog was barely even an inconvenience. She clicked the final piece in place, extended the extendable hose, attached the shoulder strap and flicked the power switch ON. 'OK, darlings, let's go fishing,' she said, and led the way up the beach.

A Sticky End

With all 441 goldfish swimming safely around inside Sausage-face Pete's bulging buttoned-down pockets, Spangles tipped the remaining water onto the sand and put the empty bathtub on the fire. The wet insides instantly **sizzled** into steam, which ran away to play with the fog.

'Looks plenty hot already, me old **frying pan**,' Sausage observed, his hands hovering over his pockets, ready to fling the goldfish into the hissing bathtub.

'Let's get rich!' Spangles grinned, reaching for the closest of Sausage's pockets.

'**Hold it right there!**' Wendy McKenzie yelled, aiming her candyfloss hose at the two silhouettes by the foggy fire, her trigger finger twitching with anticipation. 'Hands on heads!' she ordered, like a police officer or a school teacher.

The two silhouettes did as they were told. Sausage even replied, 'Yes, miss. Sorry miss,' remembering a particularly strict headmistress. As she stepped closer, Wendy recognised Sausage as the pink-bearded sailor from the funfair. '**YOU! HOW COULD YOU?**' she demanded. 'And what happened to your **pink beard**?'

'Erm . . . It's the fog, dearest pink lady, it makes everything a little gloomy. Everything but your smile . . . ' Sausage tried his best charming, hoping she wouldn't shoot him with whatever that thing was she was pointing in his direction.

Wendy saw the bathtub on the fire and screamed, 'My fish!' She swung her hose away from Spangles and Sausage and sprayed the flames with bright pink candyfloss.

Wendy thought this would put out the fire.

Freddie thought the candyfloss would melt and make a sticky mess.

Horatio thought he was in the future.

Spangles McNasty thought this was the perfect time to make a run for it.

Freddie was correct. The candyfloss melted

instantly, being all sugar and air and not a lot else. Wendy and Horatio were wrong. Spangles was correct too. He grabbed Sausage's arm and ran, dragging him towards the only thing he could see: the lighthouse.

Freddie checked the bathtub for melted goldfish, and was very relieved to find none. Then he ran after the thieves, with Horatio and Wendy not far behind.

Spangles and Sausage charged into the lighthouse and straight up the stairs.

Being the oldest lady in Bitterly Bay and possibly the universe, Wendy McKenzie panted to a halt at the foot of the 350-step spiral staircase. 'I'll wait here, **darling**, for when they come back down,' she said and raised her candyfloss cannon in readiness.

Freddie leapt up the stairs three at a time as Philip Go-Lightly shot past in the **opposite direction**, sliding down the handrail. 'Oh! More people for the picnic. Lovely. I'll put extra chips on,' he called, his voice trailing off as he descended.

Spangles and Sausage were almost at the top when Spangles realised his mistake and saw the dead end approaching. 'Don't suppose you've got a couple of parachutes tucked away in that yellow mac of yours, Sausage?' he asked as the light came into view.

'Don't be daft, me old lampshade. What would a sailor need a parachute for?' Sausage replied, reaching the top of the stairs first and running behind the huge revolving light.

'What would a sailor need a sofa and a measuring jug for?' Spangles whispered, joining his friend in hiding.

'For sitting and measuring of course,' Sausage answered as if it was perfectly normal to carry a blow-up sofa and a plastic jug everywhere with you.

Freddie charged onto the lighting platform and ran around the light.

If you should ever happen to find yourself playing hide-and-seek in a lighthouse, don't try hiding behind a huge, completely see-through, glass light bulb, you'll be found quicker than you can say, 'Hey, this is a lighthouse, not a land with its own sun.' Which coincidentally, is exactly what Spangles McNasty said at that very moment.

Horatio followed Freddie. He was too excited about being fifty years into the future to think of doing anything more useful, such as going the other way round the light and cornering the thieves.

Spangles and Sausage ran out, leapt onto the handrail and slid all the way back down to ground level. 'Pass me the torch, Sausage,' Spangles said as they approached the end of the ride. 'We need to find our boat in the fog, and FAST.'

Spangles was so busy picturing his glorious escape on his newly collected golden boat with all of his goldfish collection intact in Sausage's pockets, and maybe even finding somewhere quiet for them to grow as big as whales, he had forgotten all about the lady with the candyfloss cannon.

Wendy McKenzie had not forgotten about him. As he flew off the end of the handrail, she sprayed him and Sausage with a jet of bright pink, deliciously sticky candyfloss.

They staggered past Wendy, through the door, and onto the beach. She followed and continued spraying. By now Sausage and Spangles were stuck together inside a growing ball of pink candyfloss and stumbling forwards like contestants in a blindfolded three-legged race.

'The fog's gone pink!' Sausage cried. 'I can't see a thing!'

'If we can just get to the sea, we can wash it off,' Spangles said.

'The fog?'

'The candyfloss!'

Sausage wriggled his lips a little and munched a piece of the pink fog. It was delicious. 'We could eat our way out!' he said happily.

Wendy sprayed even more candyfloss over his

head. 'You could try, darling,' she said, chuckling to herself.

'Oh lovely, a candyfloss machine, can I have a go?' Philip Go-Lightly asked, as he ran down the beach with Freddie and Horatio. 'This is turning into quite a picnic!' Philip grabbed the candyfloss cannon hose and accidentally sprayed candyfloss all over everyone but himself.

Spangles and Sausage **hobbled** onto the jetty trying to see through their thick pink blindfolds.

'Hey! Don't leave now.' Philip dropped the hose and grabbed Sausage's mac by its very pink, very sticky collar. 'The fun's only just begun!'

'The Fish of Gold, Sausage, it's got to be here somewhere!' Spangles urged and desperately tried to drag Sausage-face Pete further along the jetty.

'The chips are **almost ready**!' Philip yelled back, realising he had never been so happy in his life: maybe he did like people after all.

Wendy switched off the candyfloss cannon and tried to wipe the candyfloss from her face, but only made it worse. Horatio did the same, suggesting, 'If we all get on my jet ski, we could pop back into the past and stop Philip before he sprays candyfloss everywhere.'

Freddie ran to join the tug-of-war on the jetty, thrusting his **sticky hands** into the pink ball of thieves and grabbing Sausage's collar too.

Sausage had an idea. 'A sailor is always prepared,' he said, remembering he always wore two yellow fisherman's macs, one on top of the other, in case he ever found himself in a particularly sticky situation such as this.

As Philip and Freddie struggled to drag him back onto the beach, Sausage-face Pete ducked towards them, letting them pull the candy covered mac off over his head. Freddie and Philip fell backwards, landing in a sticky heap on the jetty, with the pink yellow mac on top of them.

Spangles tottered backwards in the opposite direction, flailing at Sausage. He clutched a fistful of new clean mac and **pulled** Sausage off the side of the jetty.

They both hit the water with a hard **CLUNK** and quickly realised they were in a rowing boat and not the sea. Each grabbing an oar with a sticky pink hand, they heaved the boat away from the jetty. Rowing away from the shore and away from Rock Bank, they washed candyfloss from their faces with sea water as they made their escape.

'**QUICK!** To the jet ski!' Horatio suggested, charging into the sea with Wendy.

Freddie noticed the water leaking from the mac's bulging pockets and **peeked** inside one of them.

'Wait. Mrs McKenzie,' he said. 'Your fish are in here.'

'Here in the future?' Horatio asked.

'Are they . . . ? Have they . . . ?' Wendy couldn't quite bring herself to say it.

'No, they're fine, look.' Freddie showed Wendy a pocket full of fish, swimming in contented tiny circles.

'Oh goody!' Philip clapped his hands together. 'Let's get them on the fire! The chips are nearly done.'

'You'll do no such thing!' Wendy said, sloshing out of the shallows and examining the mac.

She quickly **whipped** a small plastic bag from her own pocket and scooped one of the goldfish into it.

'Here you go, Freddie,' she said, her face full of joy and candyfloss as she handed him the bag. 'I think you've earned it.'

Now all he had to do was be the best goldfish owner his mum had ever seen and a pet upgrade seemed inevitable. '**Thank you**, Mrs McKenzie.'

Freddie beamed, taking his new not-at-all-solid-gold-but-orange-coloured fish. He looked out at the fog-filled sea. 'Do you think they'll be back?'

'Well, you know what they say,' Philip Go-Lightly replied with the wisdom of a recluse who has spent fifty years alone, quietly contemplating life, the universe and everything. 'Probably.'

Fish Another Day

'But what about the *Fish of Gold*?' Sausage asked when they were clear of the island.

'Did you ever hear the old expression, "**He who runs off and don't get caught, lives to collect another day**"?' Spangles mused wisely.

'Not sure you can collect days as such,' Sausage said, after giving the matter some thought.

Spangles decided to ignore Sausage and

announced a new plan to save him the trouble of thinking for himself. 'So here's the new plan, Sausage. We rows back to **Bitterly Bay**, stroll innocently back to the **camper**, put all them goldies what's swimming around in your pockets back in the paddling pool and then find a nice, quiet, **nutter-free zone**, to melt 'em down. And then when we're good an' rich, we'll have a little think about how to steal the *Fish of Gold* all over again.'

With all the commotion on the jetty, Spangles hadn't noticed that Sausage had slipped out of his candyfloss-covered yellow mac (the one with the bulging pockets), leaving behind just his slightly smaller, **candyfloss-free** mac. The one with nothing at all in the pockets.

But he noticed now.

His horrified screams echoed all the way back to Bitterly Bay where Mayor Jackson had just got off the phone to Philip Go-Lightly. The Mayor had been somewhat surprised to hear the reclusive lighthouse-keeper's voice, and completely delighted to hear his precious *Fish of Gold* was safe and sound. He phoned Marjory to arrange its return.

After ten rings Marjory finally answered, sounding rather frightened. 'Hello, is there anybody there . . . ?' she asked nervously. Marjory hadn't left the Mayor's beach hut office all day, just in case she bumped into a haunted ice-cream cone, or some spooky candyfloss. 'Are you the ghost of the apple pie?' she asked.

'No, Marjory, it's me, Mayor Jackson.'

'**Oh good**. Mayor Jackson. Just the chap,' Marjory said, pulling herself together a little. 'Could you please make sure there are no haunted pies, spooky hot dogs or ghostly ice lollies in Bitterly Bay? Maybe we should go on the show, you know, on **SPOOKY COOKY**. I think it would be good for tourism, don't you **agree**?'

'On second thoughts, Marjory, I'll make the arrangements myself.' Mayor Jackson hung up his phone again, and looked out over his beloved Bitterly Bay. Philip had said nothing about what became of the thieves. The Mayor was

166

suddenly overwhelmed with the **hooba-jarbars**, or was it the **heebie-jeebies**? He never could remember. Whatever it was, it made him want to run away, but he didn't know where to.

Rain clouds had been looming over the bay all afternoon, queuing behind the fog, waiting patiently for their turn at being the **weather**. The thunder clapped, the rain fell down and hurt its knee, got up again and cried big fat rain drops all over Bitterly Bay for a **week**.

A week in which Mayor Jackson unveiled his new boat, the *Fish of Gold* (again), Wendy McKenzie decided to have another day off, Philip Go-Lightly lost his voice from non-stop **shouting**, Horatio Spectacles bought himself a new calendar and wrote *You are here* on it each morning at breakfast time, Sausage-face Pete bought another bright yellow mac, and Freddie was given a week's worth of free goes on Wendy's goldfish stall, with which he won absolutely nothing.

It was also a week in which Spangles McNasty wondered why it was that no one else had ever tried melting down goldfish to make themselves rich and decided to check the fishy facts in Bitterly Library before collecting any more. He was surprised to learn that no matter how shiny or golden they appear, goldfish are in fact made of fish, not gold. This upsetting revelation made him do the **biggest fart** of his library-trumping life.

(((Paaarp!)))

Which cheered him up immediately.

On returning to his camper-van home he found a letter **clamped** under the windscreen wiper. It was a letter from his Aunt Nugget's solicitor informing him Aunt Nugget had left him something in her will. Spangles did not know what a will was. Apart from an 'I *will* collect spangly things' or an 'I *will* fart in the library.'

The letter went on to say there would soon be a **'Will Reading'**, which would reveal who would be the new owner of the **Tunnel of Doom**. He liked the sound of that and decided to try it out. **'THE TUNNEL OF DOOOOOOM!'** he shouted happily through the camper-van window at a passing lady with a baby. The lady frowned and the baby **giggled**.

The engine grumbled its annoyance at being

started so early in the morning as Spangles turned the key in the ignition. His eyebrows did a little dance. 'Well, Trevor,' he said to Trevor, his only remaining goldfish, as the camper lurched down the road coughing thick clouds of unspeakable **FILTH** from its rusty exhaust. 'Turns out you're a rubbish orange fish and not a solid-gold whale at all. But even so, me old dullard, you know what I think?' Spangles McNasty waited a polite second or two for Trevor's response, but Trevor wasn't listening, he was too busy pretending to be a shark. 'This is going to be a right super spangler of a day.' Spangles grinned. 'I can just feel it.'

Look out for more
bonkers adventures in

THE DRAGONSITTER DISASTERS

JOSH LACEY

Illustrated by Garry Parsons

Dear Uncle Morton,
You'd better get on a plane right now and come
back here. Your dragon has eaten Jemima.

When Eddie agrees to look after his uncle's
dragon, he soon realises it's not going to be as
easy as he'd thought.

From blazing curtains and missing
pets to a firework catastrophe,
this fabulously funny collection
of three Dragonsitter stories will
have you roaring for more!

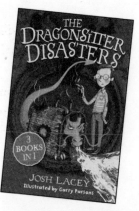

9781783441228 £6.99